To Barbara, who creates with beautiful colores, and Veni, who loves bollilos,
chocolate, and helping friends learn Español—R. G. T.

For my art teacher Steve Love and art mentor Larry Carroll—J. P.

Library of Congress Cataloging-in-Publication Data:

Names: Thong, Roseanne, author. | Parra, John, illustrator.
Title: One is a pinata / by Roseanne Greenfield Thong ; illustrations by John Parra.
Description: San Francisco, California : Chronicle Books LLC, [2019]
Numbers in English and Spanish. Includes Spanish words throughout.
Summary: In rhyming text, Hispanic children count the things, like pinatas
and maracas, that can be seen in their neighborhood.
Identifiers: LCCN 2018013833 | ISBN 9781452155845 (alk. paper)
Subjects: LCSH: Hispanic Americans—Juvenile fiction. | Counting—Juvenile
fiction. | Spanish language—Vocabulary. | Stories in rhyme. | CYAC:
Stories in rhyme. | Hispanic Americans—Fiction. | Counting. | Spanish language—Vocabulary.
Classification: LCC PZ8.3.T328 Or 2019 | DDC [E]—dc23
LC record available at https://lccn.loc.gov/2018013833

Manufactured in China.

Design by Amelia Mack.
Typeset in Brandon Grotesque.
The illustrations in this book were rendered in paint.

10 9 8 7 6 5 4 3 2 1

Chronicle Books LLC
680 Second Street, San Francisco, California 94107

Chronicle Books—we see things differently. Become part of our community at www.chroniclekids.com.

ONE
Is a
PIÑATA

A Book of Numbers

By Roseanne Greenfield Thong
Illustrated by John Parra

chronicle books · san francisco

1

one ○ uno

One is a rainbow.
One is a cake.
One is a **piñata** that's
ready to break!

Two are **maracas**
we shake to the beat.
Two are **zapatos**
on my feet.

2

two ● dos

Two are the goalies.
Two are the teams.
Two are **sonrisas**
and cold ice creams!

Three are **burbujas**
that slide and wiggle—
three are the pops, and
then the giggles.

3

three ❖ *tres*

4

four ❂ cuatro

Four are **bolillos**
just waiting to dip
in four cups of chocolate—
but first take a sip!

Five are **cometas**
   that dip and fly.
Five are the **nubes** that float
   through the sky.

5

five ❂ cinco

Five beach **palapas.**
Five boats in the bay.
Five hammocks swinging
on a lazy day.

Six kinds of **salsa**
to pour on rice.
Six rosy faces from
all the spice!

Six flavored **aguas**
to quench our thirst—
try **horchata** or **piña** first!

6

six ☀ seis

Seven are marigolds
to lead the way.
Seven **calaveras** to put on display!

7

seven ☀ *siete*

Eight are the **frutas**
we eat on a stick
with chili and lime juice—
come take your pick!

8

eight ☀ *ocho*

9

nine ● nueve

Nine **paraguas**
and puddles for splashing.
Nine slick raincoats for those
who love dashing!

10

ten ✦ diez

Ten glowing **velas**.
Ten banners bright.
Ten **faroles** that guide
us by candlelight.

Ten are my friends
who join the **fiesta**.
Ten are the yawns before
our **siesta**!

1 2 3 4 5

There are so many numbers
we love to **contar**,

6 7 8

9 10

from uno to diez—
can *you* count that far?

GLOSSARY

AGUAS FRESCAS (AH-gwahs FREHS-cahs): Cold drinks made with pureed fruit, flowers, cereal, or seeds, and blended with sugar and water. Aguas frescas are often served from large glass barrels and poured out with a large ladle. Popular flavors include tamarindo (tamarind seed), horchata, mango, pineapple, and jamaica (hibiscus tea).

BOLILLOS (boh-LEE-yohs): Small oval-shaped loaves of bread, eaten throughout Mexico, Central America, and South America. Often baked in a stone oven, the bolillos' crunchy crusts and soft insides make them a favorite for dipping into cups of hot chocolate.

BURBUJAS (buhr-BOO-hahs): Bubbles.

CALAVERAS (cah-lah-VEHR-ahs): Sugar skulls given as gifts or tokens of love and placed on family altars for the Day of the Dead. The skulls (made of hard, compacted, granulated sugar) are decorated with colored sugar frosting and often have names on the foreheads.

COMETAS (coh-MEH-tahs): Kites.

CONTAR (kohn-TAHR): To count (verb).

FAROLES (fahr-OH-lehs): Lanterns made of colorful paper with a lit candle inside. They are used for nine nights before Christmas during Las Posadas, when processions walk through the village and participants stop at different homes to sing carols and enjoy food.

FIESTA (fee-EHST-ah): A celebration, party, or event with festivities.

FRUTAS (FROO-tahs): Fruit.

HORCHATA (hohr-CHAH-tah): A traditional cold drink made of ground almonds, sesame seeds, or rice with milk, vanilla, cinnamon, and sugar.

MARACAS (mah-RAH-kahs): Rattles made from dried gourds attached to a wooden handle and filled with seeds or dried beans. Maracas are shaken in pairs as rhythm instruments.

NUBES (NOO-bays): Clouds.

PALAPAS (pah-LAH-pahs): Simple shelters made from woven grass or palm tree leaves, which give shade at a beach or park.

PARAGUAS (pahr-AH-gwahs): Umbrellas.

PIÑA (PEEN-yah): Pineapple.

PIÑATA (peen-YAH-tah): A container made from papier-mâché, covered with colorful paper, and filled with candy or toys. Breaking a hanging piñata is a favorite party game: Blindfolded children take turns hitting the piñata with a stick until the treats drop to the ground. Piñatas come in different shapes, such as animals, trucks, soccer balls, unicorns, and cartoon characters.

SALSA (SAHL-sah): A sauce typically made from tomato and chilies, and poured over dishes such as eggs, meat, chicken, tacos, enchiladas, or snacks. It is also used for dipping chips. Salsa comes in many styles, such as colorado (red), verde (green), mole (made with chocolate), and pico de gallo (finely chopped tomatoes, cilantro, and onions), among others.

SIESTA (see-EHST-ah): An afternoon rest or nap, taken during the hottest hours of the day in a hot climate.

SONRISAS (sohn-REE-sahs): Smiles.

VELAS (VAY-lahs): Candles.

ZAPATOS (zah-PAH-tohs): Shoes.